THIS WORLD HAS SEEN ENOUGH SUPERHEROES.
TIME FOR THE MONSTER TO AWAKEN.

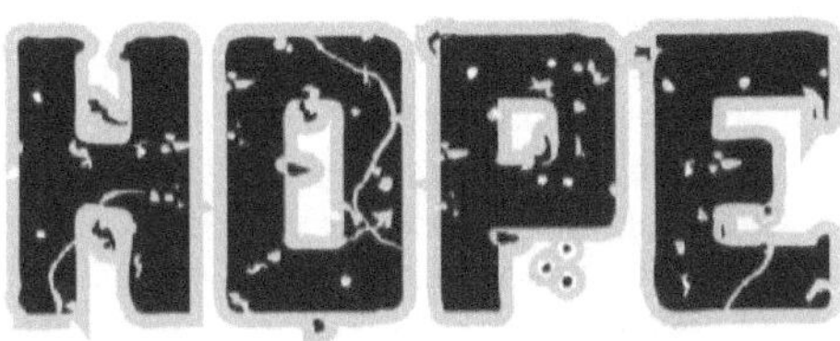

CHAPTER 1 HIGH MELTING POINT

SURIYA.B

For the one who gave me the courage to write
When my heart was heavy and the silence was
loud.

A Special Thanks to
My co-writer
Jeeva Priyan.V

"People usually look for someone to acknowledge their skills, but they often forget to acknowledge themselves.

So, I choose to acknowledge myself for writing this book."

It is the year 2326AD Mumbai has changed a lot because of climate change. The sea has risen and swallowed parts of the city. Big walls and floating islands were built to stop the water, but floods still come suddenly. The rainy season is no longer normal but sometimes it rains heavily for days, and other times, there is no rain for months. The heat is strong, with temperatures often over 50 degrees Celsius, making life hard for many people.

One of the most dangerous things now is the huge thunderstorms. Sometimes, thousands of lightning bolts strike the same area again and again, lighting up the sky and shaking the ground. These storms come without warning and can cause fires, power outages, and damage to buildings. To protect people, the city uses a Code Red alarm system It's a high-tech warning that detects when a big thunderstorm is coming. When the alarm sounds, people rush to safe shelters, underground bunkers, or climate-controlled buildings until the storm passes.

Some parts of the city have climate-controlled towers where rich people live safely. But most others live in crowded areas without protection from the heat, storms, and pollution. Robots and machines help with farming, cleaning, and delivering water because the weather is too dangerous to do everything by hand. People travel mostly by electric trains that run underground or by special electric vehicles because normal cars don't work well in this weather.

PROLOGUE

The city needs more and more energy every day to power air conditioners, robots, farms, and machines. Solar panels cover buildings and roads to catch sunlight, and wind turbines spin on the city's edges and on floating platforms in the sea. Fusion power plants provide energy too, but only the richest areas can afford them. Burning coal or oil is mostly gone because it pollutes the air and makes the heat worse. The government controls energy tightly, but power cuts still happen, especially in poorer areas, causing problems for those who depend on cooling or medical devices.

Life is hard, but people still find ways to celebrate with music, art, and festivals, even if many must stay indoors or join online. Some fight for fair energy access and better living conditions, while others try to protect the city from greedy companies and strict rulers.

It was night on the streets of sector 2.

Heavy rain with thunder and storm is approaching. A man runs into the heavy rain wearing a white lab coat soaked with blood. He is running into a large crowd with pain and fear. Everyone is frightened and pushes him away, and he continues running into a street.

The dogs in the street start barking at him. Under the heavy noise, he gets distracted and accidentally slips into the corner of the street.

As he slowly comes to consciousness, he sees his face in the reflection of the water. He sees his nose is broken and bleeding from his forehead. He wipes the blood coming from his nose with a loud cry.

He searches his pockets with disturbed thoughts in pain and fear. He takes out a tablet from his pocket and starts to open it, but his hands are too shaky, and he drops the tablet into a small hole for rainwater drainage.

A MAN WITH A WHITE COAT
"No… No… Why…"

The man is shouting

As thunder strikes the ground, he punches the ground and slowly looks at the dark sky. He shouts with a large amount of pain and anger, his voice matching the thunder's roar.

PART 1: THE ACCIDENT

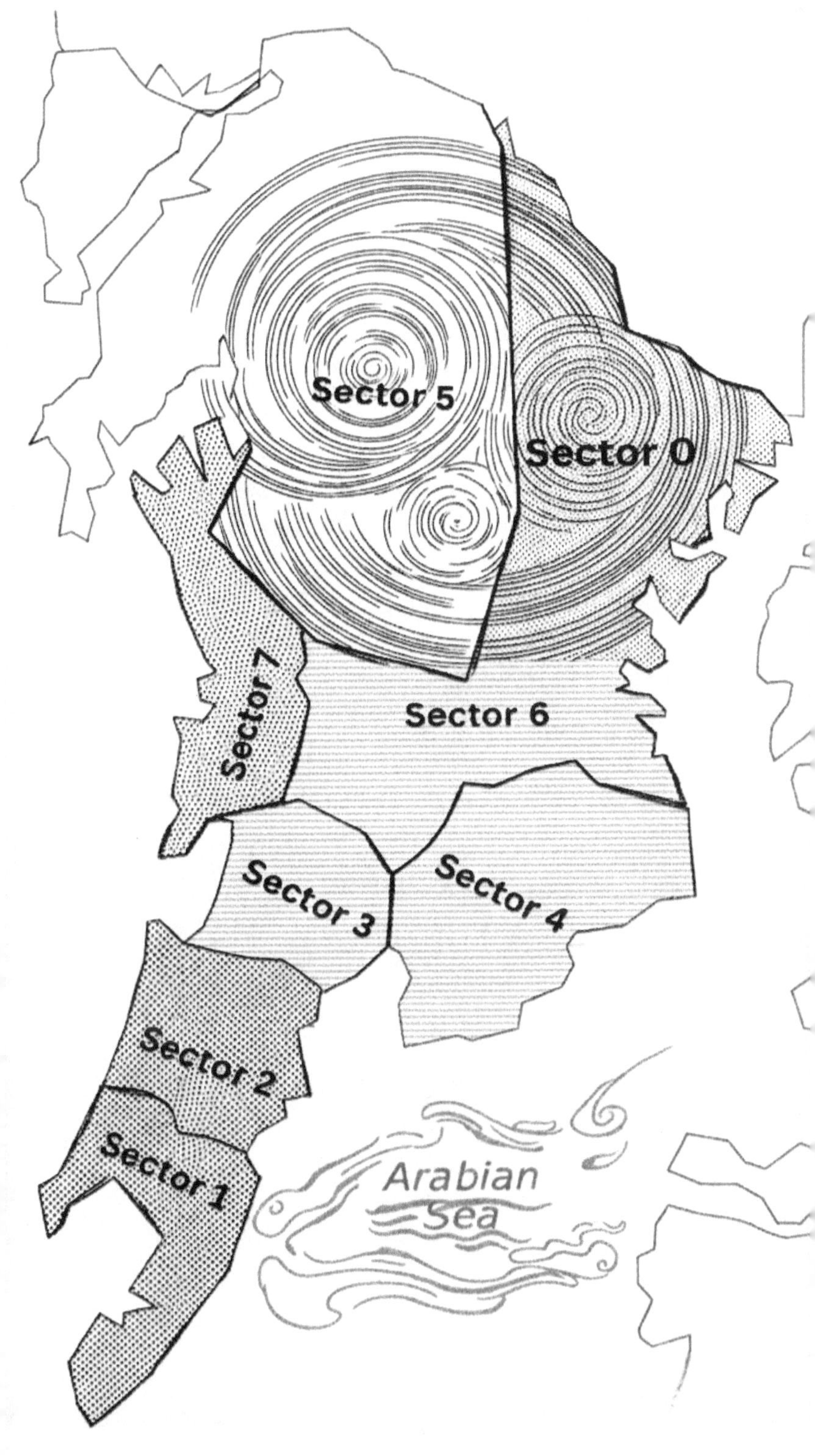

Sector 5
Sector 0
Sector 7
Sector 6
Sector 3
Sector 4
Sector 2
Sector 1
Arabian Sea

FEW MONTHS LATER

Inside the House of Hope, in the Morning

On the television, a news reporter talks about Victor Industries and their new project, the energy capacitor, which is meant to fix problems with electricity. But since the company became private, the electricity bills have become very high. As the reporter's voice fades, Anita, Hope's mother, is seen doing housework in the background. On the table, there are a few awards she has won for her work as a fashion designer.

HOPE'S MOTHER
Hope, get up soon! I made breakfast for you.

HOPE
Ohh... jeez....

she is waking up

HOPE'S MOTHER
It's your first day at your new school, and I hope you won't be late.

HOPE
Again, another one...

Outside the House

Hope comes out of the house while her mother waits for her with her bags packed in the car.

HOPE'S MOTHER
Hurry up, we are running out of time. You're going to be late today.

HOPE
Yeah, I'm coming...

She opens the car door and sits in the back seat.

HOPE'S MOTHER
Did you take a bath properly?

HOPE
Yeah...

HOPE'S MOTHER
Did you turn off all your gadgets and lights in your room? The electricity bill is getting high.

HOPE
Yes, Mom, I turned them off.

HOPE'S MOTHER
Are you wearing underwear?

HOPE
Mom... stop

HOPE'S MOTHER
What? I'm your mother. You're 16, but you haven't reached puberty yet. I'm just asking.

HOPE
Yeah, I am wearing it, thanks for asking.

Hope's mother started the car. The engine made strange sounds, like something was wrong. She waited for a second, then slowly drove out of their street.

Hope looked out of the window.

As they turned the corner, a big view of the city came into sight.

It was Mumbai, but not like before.
Tall buildings stood everywhere. They were made of shiny glass and metal. The roads were clean and wide. Small lights on the road showed the way. Electric cars moved quietly.

Robots cleaned the streets and helped people. Big screens on buildings showed news, time, and weather. People walked with smart watches that gave them directions. Trains moved fast above the roads.

"Mumbai City – 2326 AD"

On A Road In sector 3

Hope and her mother are on their way to school when they get stuck in traffic. Hope looks out the window and sees a robot slowly clearing the road. As their car starts to move, she gets a better look at the robot.

ROBOT
Beep… beep… follow the traffic rules.
Beep… beep… follow the traffic rules.

HOPE
Shit… rusted tin head.

The car starts to move again. Hope begins to narrate her story from her point of view.

(FLASH BACK)
In her previous schools, she got bad grades and did not have good relationships with others.
Because of this, her old school principal expelled her.

(PRESENT DAY}

She puts on her headphones and starts listening to music. The sounds around her begin to fade away.

Outside The School Campus

Hope gets out of the car and begins walking toward the school gate when her mother calls her from behind.

                    HOPE'S MOTHER
                 Hope, come over here!

                        HOPE
                    What, Mom?

She is using her mobile

                    HOPE'S MOTHER
        This is your first day at this school, and I
        worked very hard to get you admitted here
        because you've already been transferred to
                 eight different schools.
                So, please be a good girl.

She has headphones in her ears and is pretending to listen to her mother.

HOPE
"Cool... what did you say?"

HOPE'S MOTHER
Give me those headphones.

HOPE
Mom, give me that!
It's a rare headphone, and it's the only one
I have.

HOPE'S MOTHER
I will give it back to you after school hours.

HOPE
It's not fair.

HOPE'S MOTHER
yeah...
you've changed 8 different schools. How
about that!

She wears her hoodie, then opens the front door and is shocked to see the students in the school fighting among themselves.

                    HOPE
     Cool. I think I will barely survive here for a
                    week.

As Hope is walking into the entrance of her
class...

               RANDOM STUDENT
     His nose is bleeding! Somebody help...

                    HOPE
               Let him die!

          ANOTHER RANDOM STUDENT
               Hey, sweetie!

                    HOPE
               Fuck off!

                    YUVA
               Hey, nice jacket.

                    HOPE
               I hate this one.

YUVA
That was rude! I've never seen you here before.
What is your name? My name is Yuva.

My name
is yuva

HOPE
I'm new here. Hope.

YUVA
Well, nice to meet you, Hope. See you later!

HOPE
Asshole!

MEERA
Hi, Hope. Nice to meet you.

HOPE
Hello... Do I know you?

MEERA
Your mother told me about you. Our mothers are best friends. You have also attended my birthday parties.
(FLASH BACK)

Inside Meera's House.

Everyone is celebrating Meera's birthday. As she is about to cut the cake, Hope is busy using her mobile phone.

Suddenly, a child throws a piece of cake at her head, but she ignores it and continues using her phone.

{PRESENT TIME}

HOPE
Did I?

The bell rings.

MEERA
Come on, sit with me.

HOPE
Ohh... well... I......

Meera grabs Hope and pulls her into the classroom.
Once inside, Meera begins gossiping about the other students.

MEERA
Hey, did you see that guy talking to the other girls?

HOPE
Yeah, I'm familiar with him. He flirted with me once.

MEERA
His name is Robert Clive.

In the left corner of the class, he's trying to impress the other girls.

ROBERT CLIVE
You're the most beautiful girl I have ever seen.

NESS
Hey, yesterday you told me it was me.

ROBERT CLIVE
No darling, she is beautiful, but you are beyond that.

NESS
Really!

She is blushing

ROBERT CLIVE
Yes, darling do I look like a liar? Am I lying girls?

He is combing his hair

Girls in the crowd continue laughing.

MEERA
He's a playboy.

HOPE
Ohh… I see that.

MEERA
Hey, look at the other end, the couple sitting
over there.

HOPE
Yeah, looks like they're fighting.

MEERA
She's a drama queen. She also fights with
her boyfriend because she thinks he is
cheating on her.

On the right corner of the class, a girl is
fighting with her boyfriend.

GIRL
Where were you last night?

BOY
At my home…

GIRL
You're lying... you didn't pick up my call.

BOY
I was sleeping...

GIRL
Then you don't care about me.

BOY
God dam it...

MEERA
See that guy wearing specs? He is Jeeva, a smart boy here.

JEEVA
Hey, why are you two staring at me?

MEERA
Nothing...

HOPE
Why are you telling all this to me?

                    MEERA
            Because you're my friend!

                    HOPE
    I don't want any friends. I want to be alone.

The bell rings.
Hope moves out of the class.

                    MEERA
        Wow... I didn't see that coming.

Inside The Library

Hope is reading a comic book about Shaktiman in the library.

                    MEERA
Hey, you're here. I've been searching for you the whole time.

                    HOPE
            ohh... not again...

                    MEERA
Hey, I have a vegetable salad. I made it myself.
            Do you want some?

She is eating her salad

                    HOPE
                 No, thanks.

She takes out her phone and shows a picture
of her cat.

                   MEERA
      Look at my cat. Her name is Antenna.

                    HOPE
              Ehew... that's weird.

                   MEERA
   Today evening there's a robot fair. Can we go
                   there?

                    HOPE
             No, I have things to do.

                   MEERA
      Then tomorrow we can go to a movie.

                    HOPE
      No, I'm not coming to crowded places.
             I'm allergic to them.

MEERA
Then... where can we go?

HOPE
Hey, look, I appreciate what you're doing, but
I don't need anyone's help.

She moves outside the library.

Inside The Public Bus,

Hope was wearing headphones, sitting in the back left corner by the window, and looking outside. Outside, there were digital displays showing news about Victor Industries' new invention, the Power Capacitor.

Inside the bus, a monitor was playing a video that explained how the Power Capacitor worked.

It said that the device collected energy from lightning, changed it into electricity, and sent it to important places through underground wires.

The bus was moving on its own. When it reached her stop, it stopped automatically.

A robotic voice said, "We have reached your stop.

Sector 2."

In The Street of Sector 2, Evening.

Hope got off the bus and started walking along the platform.
She saw a group of thugs beating a man and stealing his valuables.

The man cried out for help, but she ignored him.
As she continued walking down the street, she suddenly entered a strange shop in the market area.

Inside The Shop,

She walks inside the shop and she meets a strange person purchasing strange package illegally (drugs)

HOPE
That's it

SHOP OWNER
That's all I got

HOPE
Here is the currency chips

SHOP OWNER
It's pleasure to business with you

Inside The House of Hope

She opened the door and went inside the
house. She walked up the stairs slowly.At the
top, she went to her room.
She closed the door quietly and sat down.

Inside The House of Hope

In the dining table hope and her mother is
eating where hope still uses her mobile phone

HOPE'S MOTHER
How was your day?

HOPE
Cool...it was fun

HOPE'S MOTHER
I need a help to move your dad's things to
homeless people.

HOPE
Mom,
How many time I'm telling,
don't talk about him

HOPE'S MOTHER
Hope....

HOPE
He is not my father he has abandoned us I
don't want to talk about a selfish man.

She walked away from the dining area and
went to her room.

Hope's mother cried with strong feelings.

Inside The Classroom

Hope sat in the last corner of the class and
wrote something in her notebook.
Suddenly, Meera came up to Hope.

MEERA
Hello, hope

HOPE
God damn it ...

She is breathing heavily

Hello, hope
There is my nightmare,
when it's going to stop

She is opening her lunch box and eating her sandwich

MEERA
Do you want some?

Hope
No thanks!

Suddenly, the teacher entered the class.
Meera quickly hid her food box under the table.

TEACHER
It's a lovely day

RANDOM STUDENT
For what sir?

TEACHER
For the exam...

HOPE
Ohh... great!

BELL RINGES
Everyone submits their answer sheets hope also submits and moves out of the class

TEACHER
Hope.... come over here
Your performance is too poor and your
grades are not good so you need to work
hard understand

HOPE
Yeah....cool, bye dude

She put her headphones in her ears and
started to walk away from the class.

TEACHER
Dame.... This generation has no manners

Outside The Classroom

Hope walked out of the class and accidentally
bumped into a thug named Jason at school.

HOPE
I didn't do this on a purpose it is purely an
accident

MEERA
Yeah,it was an accident

JASON
How dare you? you're not going to forget
this

MEERA
Hope! I know how to handle this situation,
run....

JASON
Where are you going? You're not going to
escape from jason

They both ran to the dead end of the corridor.
Jason came from behind them, and his
shadow covered them both.

MEERA
I'm happy to die with my friend

HOPE
I'm not your friend

MEERA
After our death we will go to heaven and i will
be with you forever in heaven.

HOPE
"You're not going to leave me there too."

JASON
Shut up! I'm going to kill you both

MEERA
Then kill hope first she's my best friend she
can't live without me

HOPE
I never said that

MEERA
Do it quickly we are going to see the blue
angel in the heaven

Jason was irritated by both he tries to punch
both
Meera and hope
Suddenly Yuva interrupted.

YUVA
Leave them Jason

JASON
What did you say?

YUVA
I told u to leave them, come on, it's not
worth!

"He is slowly moving toward Yuva, breathing heavily with frustration."

                    MEERA
              He is very brave

She is blushing

                    JASON
            You think you're a hero?
           Let me show you who I am.

                    YUVA
       Hey, take it easy i don't want to fight

He grabbed his shirt

                    JASON
          I am gonna kick your ass

He started hitting Yuva, and Yuva couldn't fight back because he was too big and strong.

                    HOPE
            It's the time to escape

MEERA
You can't leave him he is fighting for us

HOPE
I didn't asked

Students in the corridor of the school started
making noise, chanting,

'Jason... Jason... Jason...'

Yuva's eyes are swollen and his chin is hurt.
He holds his fists, but he doesn't want to fight.
He just wants Jason to stop hitting him.

MEERA
He is punching him...

HOPE
I don't care. I'm leaving this place.

MEERA
You're a selfish

HOPE
"Yeah, just like everyone else in the world
pretending to care, but walking away anyway."

She started to leave the school. Meera watches Hope leaving through the back entrance.
Meanwhile, Yuva is still fighting with him.

Large crowd cheering and taking pictures Loser.....loser.... loser...

In the large crowd Robert Clive and his girlfriend.

NESS
Robert, you said you're a boxer.
Go and help him!

"I just said that to impress her," he thought to himself.

ROBERT CLIVE
Baby, I want to help him, but today is a full moon day, so I can't fight. If it weren't for that, I would have knocked him down.

Brainless
barbarians

At the corner of the corridor, Jeeva is reading a chemistry book while observing everything around him.

JEEVA
Brainless barbarians!

He is also moving outside of the school

Inside the school's sports store and dressing room,

After some time, Yuva packed his things, getting ready to move out of the school. Meera approached him, trying to comfort him.

MEERA
Hey, hi are you okay?

They're walking into the Changing room

YUVA
Yeah, I'm okay but my handsome face is broken

Both are laughing Meera is blushing they Stopped moving they're seeing each other

MEERA
You're a cricket player

YUVA
Yeah, but..... not very good at that

Suddenly, a red alarm began ringing both in the building and on their mobile phones.

Meera checked her phone and saw that a thunderstorm was approaching. They quickly moved toward the school basement.

THUNDERSTORMS ARE NATURAL PHENOMENA. THEY OCCUR DUE TO ATMOSPHERIC CHANGES IN WEATHER CONDITIONS. DURING A THUNDERSTORM, THOUSANDS OF LIGHTNING STRIKES CAN HIT THE SAME AREA WITHIN A SHORT PERIOD, OFTEN ACCOMPANIED BY HEAVY RAINFALL.
SO, THE CITY CREATED UNDERGROUND BUNKERS AND A THUNDERSTORM ALERT SYSTEM TO FORECAST WEATHER. LIGHTNING RODS WERE INSTALLED ON EVERY BUILDING TO SAFELY REDIRECT LIGHTNING STRIKES TOWARD THE OCEAN.

Street of Sector 2

Hope was walking down the street when a red alarm suddenly began ringing everywhere, including on everyone's mobile phones.
Panic spread instantly. People were frightened and started running toward the basements of nearby buildings.

Hope looked up at the sky, a storm was approaching.

                    HOPE
                  Ohh...no...

She started running toward the large crowd

FEW MINUTES EARLIER

Inside Riya's Research Centre

A man looks toward a thunder power plant, and a voice comes from behind him.

                    RIYA
                 Edward .....

EDWARD
Hey, Riya

RIYA
"Are you still thinking about the case?
we already filed against Victor?
Don't worry."

EDWARD
I still can't believe he betrayed me, I trusted
him

RIYA
Leave him, come with me I'll show you
something

They are walking towards the large mirrored
box where many plants are preserved in
containers. Riya is a botanist.

RIYA
Here look at this

EDWARD
What is this?

RIYA
Well, that's a great question, but I don't have
an exact answer. It's a normal, looking plant
like any other, but it has the ability to absorb
radiation and regenerate.

EDWARD
How is this possible?

RIYA
Yeah, I know. This plant gene was taken
from
Hiroshima, where the first nuclear bomb was
dropped nearly 3 centuries ago and now that
place has recovered and evolved.

EDWARD
I've never seen anything like this before.
What are you trying to do with it?

RIYA
Look at this plant, it has a high regeneration
ability.
If we can understand this, we could potentially
cure many diseases, including cancer.

EDWARD
"Wait a second, it's a crime
You didn't get approval from the national
research committee."

RIYA
"Well, if I am able to create a new DNA
modification in the human body, they will
accept it because it can help a lot of people.

EDWARD
Last time I tried to do something like this, it
didn't work. If they find out about this, we'll be
imprisoned, and we don't want to be involved
in anything like that. Let's just go somewhere
just you and me.

She walks toward him and holds his cheeks.

RIYA
Hey, nothing is going to happen.
I'm not going anywhere. I'm here with you.

EDWARD
Yeah, I know that, but......

RIYA

Look, I have a job for you. I'm moving inside
the radiation room to collect more samples,
and it's highly radioactive in there. Take my
ring, and promise me you will give it back to
me when I return.

EDWARD

"Yeah, I promise, till my last breath, I will hold
this for you."

She was wearing a radiation protection suit as
she moved inside the room, carefully
collecting more samples of the plant (Project
SR26) she had artificially grown inside the
mirror box.

On the other side of the transparent door, he
was watching her. She noticed and smiled
softly while he observed her.

Suddenly, an alarm started ringing loudly. The
entire laboratory locked down due to a power
fluctuation, and she found herself trapped
inside.

Edward panicked and ran toward the door,
desperate to get out.

EDWARD
Is there any emergency exit

RIYA
What? I can't hear you

EDWARD
Hey, I'm going to break this door down and get
you out, okay?

A thunderstorm began, and hundreds of
lightning strikes started hitting the ground.

Inside The Thunder Power Plant

A laser rod system was placed on each
lightning arrester to attract lightning. The
energy from the lightning passed through a
capacitor and was stored in an underground
room.

But then, a very powerful lightning strike hit the
poles. They started to melt and became
unstable.
The storage capacitor began to overload.

Street of Sector 4

The thunderstorm started to weaken, and the storm slowly moved towards the ocean.

Everyone came out of the basement and began walking back to their homes. Droids started clearing the crowd.

Hope tried to call her mom, but the signal was weak because of the storm. At the same time, Hope's mother was driving around in her car, trying to find Hope and calling her again, even though the signal wasn't working properly.

Hope started walking alone. She saw a signboard— it said "Sector 4," where the Riya Search Centre is located. The thunderstorm had caused a massive power cut.

Inside Riya's Research Centre

He tried to break the mirror box. It caused a small crack, but he couldn't break it.

Outside, a droid was moving toward them.

DROID
Sir... is there any problem?

EDWARD
K1....., help me break this door!

K1 started to break the door.

Inside The Thunder Power Plant

The power storage containers began to overload and caused a massive power blast. (Boom...!)
Electrical energy scattered through the underground pipes and spread into the underground electrical system.

Inside Riya's Research Centre
K1 was still trying to break the door. Inside the mirror room, the floor began to crack.

Cracking sounds from the floor

Due to the power fluctuations, the droid couldn't move properly.

EDWARD
No... not now!

K1
I... can't... move...

Edward   grabbed a metal rod from the room and tried to break the door himself. Inside, Riya   started to panic as electrical sparks began hitting her protective suit.

Riya is shouting in pain

EDWARD
No! I'll save you!

Suddenly, K1 powered back up and broke the door, rushing in to save Riya. But as he moved, electrical sparks struck him, damaging his system. The droid collapsed to the ground.
Riya looked up and saw the gamma container and
shocked. Her suit was half melted, and the electrical sparks began reacting with the gamma radiation.
The sparks started to glow green.

(Boom... Explosion)

Edward   screamed and ran toward her, but green electrical sparks hit him.

Half of his face was burned. One green spark struck his chest and spread across his body. His eyes began to glow. (in slow motion)
The building started to collapse as green electrical sparks rushed through the underground pipes.

Street Of Sector 4

Hope was going back to her home.
As she walked, droids were clearing the crowd.

Droid 1 "Please move quickly."
Droid 2 "Don't go that way! That area is completely blocked!"

Suddenly, the ground started shaking.
People got scared and began running everywhere. Bright green sparks came out from the underground pipes.

Hope felt afraid. She ran toward the research centre.
Then, the shaking suddenly stopped.

A loud explosion happened far away.

She turned and saw a building on fire. Green sparks were coming from it.

She looked down and realized she was standing on a water filtration pipe.
The same green sparks started coming out of the pipe under her.

The green sparks hit her body from all sides.
Her eyes started glowing slowly.
Then she fell down and became unconscious.

ENERGY MANIPULATION
LEVEL 4 – BLUE CURRENT
ENERGY MANIPULATION IS THE SOURCE OF PURE ENERGY AND ELECTRICITY. HE CAN CONTROL ALL FORMS OF ENERGY, AS WELL AS ABSORB AND PROJECT IT.

PART 2: THE RISE OF SUPERIOR

Inside The Hospital

She got the nightmare about the accident she slowly come to conscious her mother sitting beside her

                    HOPE
                  My head....

try to standup from bed

                 HOPE'S MOTHER
Hope.... you're awake I was afraid.....with tears

                    HOPE
                What happened?

                 HOPE'S MOTHER
        You been unconscious for 2 days

                    HOPE
        What?...breathing shockingly
        Droids entering into the room

                    DROID
                She is awake....

HOPE'S MOTHER
Yeah.....

DROID
Let me check her, I think something wrong
with the machine

HOPE'S MOTHER
What happened?

DROID
Her heartbeat readings showing more than
250 beats per minute

HOPE
What? Fucking tin head

HOPE'S MOTHER
Hope.... be careful with your words

HOPE
Yeah, cool...

Again unconscious

Inside The Hospital Mortuary Night

Inside the mortuary two persons where fighting for a ring

Riya's ring

PERSON 1
Hey that's mine I found the body

PERSON 2
You found body but I found the ring

Suddenly, the lights flickered in the room.

Blue sparks appeared around Edward 's dead body.His eyes slowly opened and started glowing blue.

At the same time, the power went out.

Both of them began to panic.

PERSON 2
"What's going on?"

His eyes were glowing, and blue sparks were moving all around his body.

EDWARD
Give me...... that........ ring

PERSON 1
What ring?

They're in fear

Suddenly he gives a creepy look at them

Street of sector 5 night

He was wearing a black cloak, and there was blood on his body. His eyes were glowing blue.

He walked through the busy street in Sector 5. People moved quickly around him, talking loudly. Many were speaking about the accident that happened two days ago.

He looked at them in shock.

EDWARD
Two days...

He kept walking toward Sector 5.

Suddenly, a news broadcast appeared on a large screen nearby.

It showed footage of the explosion from two days ago. The accident was caused by a container of high gamma radiation. It was linked to Riya's secret research on human DNA modification. The explosion happened because of her mistake and she died in it. Now, the head of Vector Industries was speaking about the incident.

The crowd started gossiping about the news.

Edward listened quietly, hearing every word they said.

RANDOM PERSON
She is a fucking bitch
because of her explosion happened

RANDOM PERSON
"I couldn't use my phone for hours because of her!"

He looked around at the large crowd. His eyes were strange, cold.
Small sparks of electricity came from his fingers. The floor under his feet started to crack.

People in the crowd began talking badly about her again.

RANDOM WOMAN
I'm glad she's dead.

He was losing control.

EDWARD
"No more..."

His eyes started to glow. A strong laser beam shot out from them and hit the big news screen. It exploded. Fire spread everywhere.

People screamed and started running.

Behind him, a building was on fire.

He walked out of the flames slowly, with a scary look on his face.

He looked like someone who had lost everything.
And now, he was ready to destroy everything else.

EDWARD

"This world sees you as a monster. So, let it be. It doesn't need heroes anymore... only monsters."

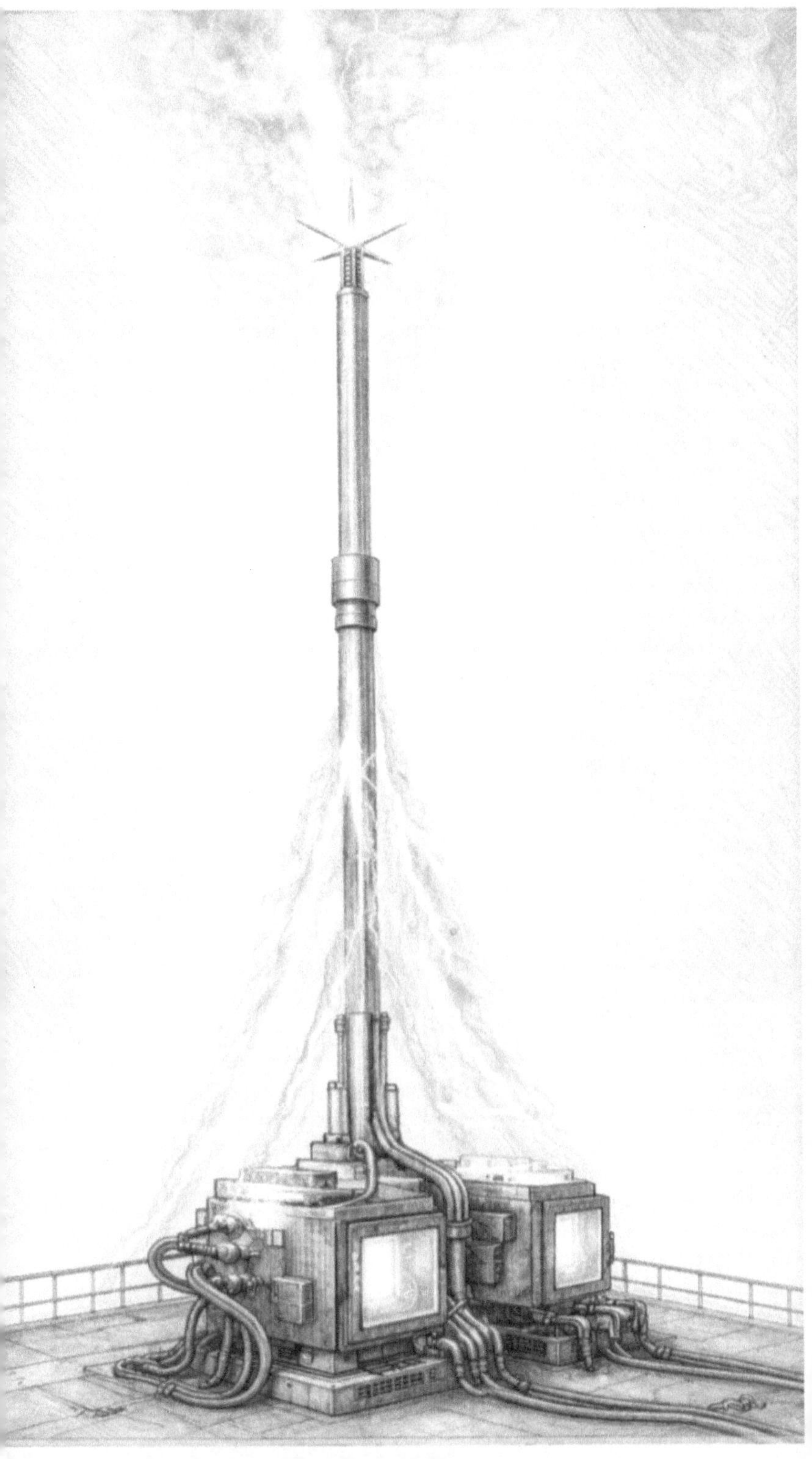

Thunder Power Plant Night

ENGINEER

Sir, these storage containers were too weak.
That's why the explosion happened.

VICTOR

Hey, keep your voice down! I don't want the
whole city to hear this.

ENGINEER

What should we do now, sir?

VICTOR

"Just cover it up. I already blamed everything
on Riya. She's dead now, and no one's going to
find out the truth. I've asked the government
for funds we'll replace them with better
containers."

Low voice, from the shadows

EDWARD

"No one knows... yet."

A quick, shadowy movement in the dark

VICTOR
"Who's there? Guards! Go check and bring that person to me!"

GUARDS
"Yes, boss!"

The guards rush out. Gunshots and screams echo from outside.

VICTOR
"Who are you?! Show yourself!
Do you even know who I am?!"

Outside, Edward slowly stepped into view, walking through the rain. Every time his foot touched the ground, the water sizzled and turned into steam. Even the raindrops disappeared before they could land on his skin.

Steam rose up from the ground and wrapped around him like a glowing mist.

He kept walking, slow and calm. The steam made his black armor and cape look strange and powerful in the dark night.

His eyes were glowing bright blue.

EDWARD
"This world gives you two choices be a good person and struggle all your life, or become a villain and build a better life no matter what."

VICTOR
Edward ....is that you?

He slowly comes out from the fog and he wearing a black armour around his body and black Cape

EDWARD
No, call me THE SUPERIOR....

The engineers in the room tried to run away. He burned a running person with his laser beam. Then, with his super speed, he grabbed another person, lifted him up, and smashed his head with his left hand.

VICTOR
Oh my God...

He grabbed Victor with his super speed and slammed him against the wall. Victor could hear his heart beating loudly.

EDWARD
There is no place for a god in hell.
He is coughing, blood coming from his mouth

VICTOR
Are... you... going to... kill me?

EDWARD
No... not just a death more than that

He grabbed victor's hand he crushing it and he
is shouting in lot's of pain

Inside The Hope Bedroom Morning

Hope was sleeping in the bed when she had a
nightmare about the accident. She suddenly
woke up in fear, and the bed was broken.

HOPE
Fuck....

HOPE'S MOTHER
What is that sound coming from your room?

HOPE
Well.... nothing..

She tried to open the door, but accidentally broke the restroom door.

                    HOPE
                  What....

               HOPE'S MOTHER
         Hope... what is that I'm coming up

                    HOPE
                  No... don't

Hope's mother is on her way to her room, trying to open the door.

               HOPE'S MOTHER
              What you're doing?

                    HOPE
              I'm.... doing yoga

               HOPE'S MOTHER
            Ohh... good keep it up

On the other side, she arranged her broken things in the corner.

Corridor Of The School

Hope is getting something in her locker suddenly Meera approaches her

                    MEERA
                    Hope...

                    HOPE
            Oh... Meera, you scared me!

Meera gave a hug.

                    MEERA
        I heard you had an accident. I was really
                worried about you.

                    HOPE
                Well... thank you.

                    MEERA
        I brought you a sandwich. I made it myself.

                    HOPE
            Thanks. I'll eat it later.

Hope started to walk away.

MEERA
Why is she acting strange? Something feels
wrong...

Hope was walking to her class. Suddenly, blue
sparks came from her fingers. She got scared,
quickly hid her hands in her hoodie sleeves,
and kept walking to class.

Inside The Classroom

Inside the classroom, Hope is sitting at her
desk, trying to focus on the lesson.

TEACHER
Okay, now we are going to learn about the
reproduction of cockroaches

Robert and his girlfriend are sitting close
together. The teacher is talking about how
cockroaches reproduce. Robert leans toward
her with a small smile.

ROBERT
This is boring. Cockroaches again?
Do you want to know how humans do it?

She is smiling

NESS
Oh yeah, How?

ROBERT
Come to my house. I'll show you. Just you and me.

She laughs

NESS
You're so naughty!

ROBERT
Only with you.

They both laugh quietly. Robert holds her hand. Their faces come close. They are about to kiss when...

TEACHER
Robert! Would you like to tell the class how cockroaches kiss?

Robert and Ness quickly sit up. Ness hides her smile. Robert looks annoyed and speaks softly.

                    ROBERT
            Shit... He spoiled my chance.

                    TEACHER
              What did you say?

He is smiling

                    ROBERT
      Nothing Sir. Cockroaches don't kiss. They
                just... you know, vibe.

The class laughs.

Suddenly, blue electric sparks come out from
Hope's fingers. The classroom lights flicker
and electrical equipment starts to explode.
Everyone panics.

                     HOPE
          I want to go to the washroom!

                    TEACHER
              I don't care just go!

He's shocked by the electric burst. Hope
quickly runs out and heads to the washroom.
Inside, she tries to control her powers.

HOPE
Come on... what's wrong with me?

Meera walks into the washroom and sees blue sparks in Hope's hands. Hope is shocked, runs into a toilet stall, and closes the door.

MEERA
Hope... what's going on?

HOPE
I'm fine!

MEERA
Did you hit puberty?

HOPE
What are you talking about?

MEERA
Just open the door.

Meera tries to open the door. She accidentally breaks it and falls on Hope. A group of girls in the washroom see them. One of them takes a picture.

                    HOPE
            It's not what you think!

                RANDOM GIRL
    It's okay, we're leaving. Bye! Hey, stop taking
                pictures, let's go.

Hope gets angry and yells at Meera.

                    HOPE
    Look what happened! This is all your fault!

Meera is shocked. Hope's eyes start glowing
blue.
The lights in the room flicker and overload.

                    MEERA
                Oh no... Hope...

                    HOPE
                    What?

                    MEERA
                Your hands...

Sparks shoot out from Hope's hands again.
They look at each other and scream. Hope
rushes out of the washroom.

MEERA
You have superpowers!

HOPE
No, I'm sick!

MEERA
You're a superhero like Minnal Murali!

HOPE
Who's Minnal Murali?

MEERA
He's a superhero, just like you!

HOPE
I'm not a superhero!

Electric sparks shoot from Hope's hands again.
Lights and devices all over the school explode.
Hope runs outside in fear.

MEERA
Wait! I'm coming with you!

In the road of mumbai city afternoon

Hope and Meera are walking down a street in

Sector 2

MEERA
Can you fly?

HOPE
No...

MEERA
Are you a god?

HOPE
No...

MEERA
You must be an alien child from another
planet.

HOPE
What are you even talking about?

MEERA
I knew it... I knew it!
You're the daughter of Shaktiman!

HOPE
I'm not who you think I am.

Suddenly, some thugs start bothering an old woman nearby.

MEERA
Hope, go help her.
Use your sparkles or something!

HOPE
I don't care.

MEERA
Why are you always so rude? I just wanted to be nice to you.

HOPE
I didn't ask you to.

MEERA
Sometimes we have to make choices about what's right in life.

HOPE
Yeah, and I've chosen to mind my own business.

MEERA
You're so arrogant. Don't talk to me again!

HOPE
Then stop following me. Go away.

Hope walks alone down the street, talking to herself.

HOPE
I never asked her to care about me.
I don't care what people say about me.
This is my life, and I'll decide what to do with it.

Inside The House Of Hope Evening

Hope opens the front door, walks into the house, and heads toward her room. Her mother stops her.]

HOPE'S MOTHER
Hope, wait... come here.

HOPE
Mom, I'm tired.
I just want to sleep.

HOPE'S MOTHER
Then what is this?
I found it in your room.

She holds up a packet of drugs.

HOPE
I... just give it to me.

HOPE'S MOTHER
How long have you been taking this?
Your father is a good officer, and look at you
acting like a criminal.

HOPE
Don't talk about him.
I'm taking those pills because of him!
He left me when I needed him the most.
He's a selfish bastard!

Her mother slaps her.

HOPE'S MOTHER
Don't you dare talk about him like that!
Do you even know who he is?

FLASH BACK
In The Road Of Sector 6 Evening

HOSPITAL DAY UNDER ATTACK

Terrorists are attacking the hospital. Indian Special Forces (ISF) are trying to stop them.

ISF OFFICER 1
Over here! Shoot them!

ISF OFFICER 2
One officer is down! We need help!

HOPE'S FATHER
They want to blow up the hospital! There's a proton bomb in that ambulance! We must take it away from here!

ISF OFFICER 2
We can't! We don't know how to stop that bomb!

HOPE'S FATHER
Cover me. I will drive it away.

ISF OFFICER 2
That's too dangerous! David....

The two officers shoot to protect him. Hope's father runs to the ambulance. He gets shot in the stomach but climbs in and drives.

HOPE'S FATHER
I'm driving to Beach Road, away from people.

ISF OFFICER 3
That bomb is very dangerous. We can't help you, sir.
He is breathing hard

HOPE'S FATHER
I understand. Can you send a message to my wife?

ISF OFFICER 3
Yes, this call is being recorded.

HOPE'S FATHER
Hey... are you at home? I can't come home
today.
Something bad is happening.
I don't have much time. I never told you this,
but you are a strong woman. Be even
stronger now.

Please take care of Hope for me. I promised
her I'd come home early to play. Tell her I'm
sorry... and that I love her very much.
Don't tell her what really happened. It will
make her too sad. I will miss you too.

ISF OFFICER 3
We are sending your message.

HOPE'S FATHER
Thank you, officer...

ISF OFFICER 3
No Sir... thank you. It's an honor to speak
with you. Goodbye, sir.

EVEN IF I DIE, I WILL ALWAYS LOVE YOU. GOODBYE, HOPE...

HOPE'S FATHER
Even if I die, I will always love you.
Goodbye, Hope...

He sees the sunset on the road by the beach. He closes his eyes and remembers his daughter's smile.

(Boom.... there was a blast)

The ambulance explodes.

PRESENT TIME

Inside The House Of Hope Evening

HOPE
No... this can't be true...

She starts crying.

HOPE'S MOTHER
He didn't leave us. He died saving thousands of people. He's not selfish. He's a hero.

HOPE
Why didn't you tell me?

HOPE'S MOTHER
I got a message from your dad. He didn't want
you to be sad.

HOPE
I'm sorry... I didn't know...

HOPE'S MOTHER
I don't care what nonsense you're doing or
saying.
Why are you even standing here? Just go!

Hope's mother storms into her room, locks the
door, and cries loudly.

On The Rooftop

Hope is sitting on the edge of a tall building,
thinking about her mistakes. She remembers
something Meera told her.

**Sometimes we have to make choices about
what's right in life.**

Hope stands up, looking over the whole city.
Electrical sparks appear from her fingers.

HOPE
I know what I have to do.
I'm a superhero.

SOMETIMES WE HAVE TO MAKE CHOICES ABOUT WHAT'S RIGHT IN LIFE.
"AND I KNOW WHAT I HAVE TO DO I'M A SUPERHERO."

She jumps off the building and flies. She starts helping people.

A car loses control and is about to crash, but suddenly stops. A masked girl floats above. The driver looks up in shock. Meanwhile, Hope's mother is still upset and not speaking to her.

A building catches fire, and the masked girl helps people escape.

Outside Meera's House

Hope rings the doorbell. Meera opens the door.

                    HOPE
            I... I'm sorry.

She is smiling

                    MEERA
            Come in. I'll show you my room.

On the street

Some thugs are trying to hurt an old lady.

HOPE
Hey! Pick on someone your own size.

THUG
I'm fine with that.

HOPE
Alright then.

Her eyes glow and sparks fly from her hands.
The thugs scream and run away.

Inside Hope's House

Hope and Meera are making a superhero suit.

HOPE
No red! I hate red.

At School

Hope and Meera walk down the hallway.
Students whisper about the mystery superhero.
In the corner, Jason bullies a classmate.

JASON
Give me that!

STUDENT
That's my last one!

Hope shoots a small spark at Jason. His back catches fire, and he runs to the restroom screaming.

JEEVA
What... something's not right.

Jeeva noticed everything that was happening, and he started to follow Hope

Jason runs to the restroom yelling because his back is burning from a spark.
Robert turns to Ness with a teasing smile.

ROBERT
Looks like Jason's back is on fire.
But when I see you, my heart's the one that's burning... lucky me.

NESS
Oh wow,
Mr. Romeo. Burning heart, huh?
Is that your big line?

ROBERT
Hey, don't hate the player, hate the fire.
And trust me, it only burns for you.

She laughs

NESS
Be careful.
You might start a fire here too.

ROBERT
I hope so.
Maybe we can keep each other warm later.

NESS
I'd like that.

They are both laughing

MEERA
Disgusting……

Back at Hope's House

Hope and Meera are working on the superhero suit again.

HOPE
Who needs a red cape or a big "S" on their chest?

MEERA
Okay, no red cape. No symbols. Got it.

She writes in her notebook.

In The City Streets

Thieves rob a bank and speed away. ISF officers chase them. Hope helps stop the thieves.

Back at Hope's House

HOPE
Yes! That's the one.

She is Breathing heavily

MEERA
Finally.

At night, Hope stands on the edge of a building wearing her new suit, looking out over the city.

In The Top Of The Building Morning

Hope is sitting on the edge of a rooftop, eating.
Her phone starts ringing.
She answers her phone

                    HOPE
              Hello? Who is this?

                    MEERA
              It's Alfred speaking.

                    HOPE
      Meera, don't mess with me. Why did you
              change your number?

                    MEERA
      Seriously? Don't say my name out loud
            you're revealing my identity.

                    HOPE
            Why are you doing this?

                    MEERA
          Because I'm your sidekick.

                    HOPE
      It's... okay, but I don't want a sidekick.

MEERA
Hey, come on. Every superhero needs a
sidekick!

HOPE
Really...?

Suddenly, there's an explosion in the center of
the city. Hope stands up, alert.

HOPE
I'll call you back.

MEERA
What's going on?

Call ends

MEERA
It's sidekick time.

In The Road Of Sector 2 Morning

Hope flies through the sky and lands in a place
where rogue robots are attacking. People are
running in fear. The robots stop and start
scanning her.

ROGUE ROBOT
Target found...

Victor industries morning

A person in black armor stands inside the building.

EDWARD
I'm coming. Hold her for me.

Mumbai City Road Morning

ROGUE ROBOT
Yes, sir.

Hope starts fighting the robots.

HOPE
What are you things doing here?

ROGUE ROBOT
Attack... attack... She's destroying all units trying to stop her!

HOPE
Is that all you've got?

She easily destroys the rest of the robots.

                    HOPE
There's no one left to stop me

Suddenly, she sees something flying toward her. It's a person in black armor, watching from above.

                    HOPE
So, you're the boss? I'm going to take you down.

                    EDWARD
Try me...

Hope flies toward him and tries to punch, but he dodges quickly. She lands another punch, but it's weak.
Edward   activates Energy Manipulation

                    EDWARD
Energy Manipulation Level 1.

Blue lightning covers his body. He grabs Hope's head, flies up, and punches her into the road, then throws her into an apartment building. They start fighting inside.

Hope struggles he's too powerful.
Then he powers up again

                    EDWARD
        Energy Manipulation Level 2.

His entire body glows with electricity. Lightning surrounds his hands.

Hope becomes afraid and runs out of the building. She looks back and sees him coming. He punches toward her,she flies away. She throws a bus at him, but he punches it into pieces.

She tries to escape, but he grabs her and slams her into the ground.

                    EDWARD
        You can't run from me.

                    HOPE
    Who are you? What do you want from me?

                    EDWARD
    Shut up. I can hear your heart beating.
    Wearing fancy hoodies won't save you.

HOPE
Leave me alone!

EDWARD
I can feel your fear.

HOPE
You're lying...

His eyes glow. Lightning sparks from his
hands.
Hope starts to panic.
Her heart races.

I CAN FEEL
YOUR
FEAR

ISF officers surround the area, trying to control the situation.

                    ISF OFFICER
                  Over here... Launch!

A missile is fired at Edward . He slowly turns and punches it. The missile explodes into flames.

                    ISF OFFICER
                     He's gone!

But Edward walks out from the fire. His armor is damaged. He starts attacking the officers destroying their vehicles with super speed and laser blasts from his eyes.

Then he lifts his hand

                     EDWARD
              Energy Manipulation Level 3.

Bright lightning shoots from his palm, striking enemies and vehicles. Everything around him explodes and burns.

He also shoots a powerful laser beam from his eyes, cutting through metal and buildings.

After the attack, he notices Hope is missing. He sees an open drain nearby.

                    EDWARD
                     Fear.

A robotic voice speaks from his armor.

                    AI VOICE
Sir, your armor durability is at 40%. Should I
                 search for her?

                    EDWARD
             No. I got what I needed.

He holds a small container with a sample of Hope's hair. He flies away.

Drainage pipes

Hope is running through the dark tunnel, scared. She hears sounds behind her. Sewage water rushes in. She slips and falls into a water, filled area. She pulls herself out, wet and dirty.

She sees her reflection in the water. Her clothes are soaked. She sits in a corner, crying.

HOPE
I messed up everything...
I'm just a coward...

She is crying

Victor Industries Later

Edward   lands at the headquarters. He places the hair sample into a container. He removes his armor as he walks. His body slowly shrinks down.

He enters a healing pod. The container closes around him and begins scanning. He lies still, unconscious.

PART 3: LOVE AND BETRAYAL

I THAT
PECIAL,
WARD?
RIYA...
IN YOUR GAZE,
I SEE STORIES
THE WORLD
WILL NEVER
HAVE THE
PATIENCE TO
UNDERSTAND.

FLASH BACK

Inside The House Of Edward Morning

Alarm buzzing...
He slowly wakes up and looks at the time 7:30
AM.

                    EDWARD
              Oh no, not again...

He takes a towel and heads to the washroom.
A droid, K1 his caretaker, built by him,
Approaches from behind.

                    K1
           Sir, do you need any help?

                    EDWARD
        Find my name pin, keys, and lab coat.

He puts on his clothes and searches for his
things.

                    EDWARD
             Did you see my keys?

K1
In the left cupboard.

EDWARD
Yes, thank you. Bye!

He is stepping out of his house.

K1
Sir, you forgot

The door shuts...
K1 sees that he has already gone outside.

He is looking at his watch

EDWARD
Oh no... it's 7:45 again!

He sees a car in front of him. The car suddenly drives away. He notices an e-bike in the corner. It's powered by kinetic energy. He hops on and rides fast.

He rushes towards his college. There are many obstacles on the way.

Suddenly, the e-bike crashes into some dustbins.

                    EDWARD
          Again... I didn't see that coming.

He reaches the college and parks the e-bike in the parking area.

                    SECURITY
          Hey, where's your parking ticket?

                    EDWARD
          I'll give it to you tomorrow.

                    SECURITY
          Hey... you've been saying that for a month now!

He tries to use the lift, but it won't open.

                    EDWARD
          Come on... come on...

He keeps pressing the lift button.
He checks his watch
It's already 8:20 AM.
He quickly takes the stairs.

As he reaches the entrance of his classroom, he accidentally drops his name badge. He picks it up and walks towards the class.

EDWARD
Professor, can I come in?

PROFESSOR
Yeah, you're too early for my class. Get in. But don't disturb the class.

He walks in. No one wants to sit next to him. He looks around and quietly goes to sit in the last corner.
He takes out his notebook and pen for class.

Suddenly, the bell rings. He was too late.

PROFESSOR
Students, I want you all to write a short answer about today's class.
Edward , I want a full summary from you.

The students laugh...

College Corridor

Students are walking outside the class.

One student accidentally bumps into Edward , causing him to drop all his notes. Two other students walk by and hit him on the back of his head.

                    STUDENTS
                    Loser...

Suddenly, K1 walks over to the scene.

                    K1
          Sir, you forgot your underwear!

The crowd bursts into laughter.

                    K1 (innocently)
          Sir, did I do something wrong?

                    EDWARD (smiling slightly)
                    No, buddy. Thanks.

Library

Edward is searching for a book on aerospace engineering. He moves along the shelves, scanning the titles.

EDWARD
I got it...

Just then, a cool breeze flows in from an open window. He walks over to close it, but pauses when he notices something outside.

He sees a child playing happily with their parents. The sight suddenly triggers painful memories from his past.

In The Playground

CHILD
Daddy, I found the ball!

He throws the ball, laughing loudly.

DADDY
Go find it again!

He watches him with emotion in his eyes.

FLASHBACK

Inside The Car Night

Little Edward is sitting in the backseat, playing

with a rubber ball. His parents are arguing in
the front seats.

EDWARD 'S MOTHER
How many times do I have to tell you? Stop
drinking alcohol!

EDWARD 'S FATHER
It's just for one day.

EDWARD 'S MOTHER
You've been doing this for so long. If you
keep drinking, I'll leave you.

EDWARD 'S FATHER
Ugh... shut up! I'll do what I want. If you want
to leave, then go!

EDWARD 'S MOTHER
Then give me back the dowry you took from
my father!

He slaps her.

EDWARD 'S FATHER
Didn't you hear me?
Be quiet!

Little Edward looks up, scared, watching everything.

EDWARD
Mom...

EDWARD'S MOTHER
Nothing, sweetheart... everything's going to be fine.

Suddenly, the car crashes into a truck. Both parents die in the accident. Little Edward survives but injures his right hand.

He is Crying

EDWARD
Mom... Mom...

PRESENT TIME

The Library

Edward looked shocked. He quickly closed the windows, searched his pocket, and took out a tablet. After swallowing it, his mind calmed down. He had been struggling with psychological issues since that day.

Suddenly, someone approached him.

RIYA
Edward ...

EDWARD
Hey... come, sit here.

RIYA
How was your day?

EDWARD
Just a normal day. Can we go out?

RIYA
No,
I have work. Maybe after 8 p.m. at the train
station. And don't make me wait, okay?

She walks out of the library.

Train Station Night

They sat on a bench, talking about their college
memories. A train moved in the background.

Mumbai Street – Night

They walked down the quiet streets of Mumbai, still sharing memories.

RIYA
Look at you, soon you'll be a scientist!

EDWARD
Not really. I'm just going to graduate in Physics.
But you're already a PhD in Botany.

RIYA
Plants are important for our environment. And stop acting like I am older than you. So, what will you do after graduation?

EDWARD
I'm thinking of taking a short break with you.

RIYA
Come on, seriously. Where do you plan to work?

EDWARD
Ugh, it's all such a drag. These days,
education is just about getting
qualifications. Then, those
qualifications become the key to getting a job.
But in the end, you're working for someone
else's success, just for some money.
Slowly, you forget who you really are and
what you're truly capable of.

Then one day, you ask yourself,
Am I educated, or just a well, trained slave?

RIYA
Wow. That was deep. I'm impressed.

EDWARD
Well, I'm also good at poetry.

RIYA
Really?

EDWARD
The lightning that falls from the sky is
beautiful... But it's nothing compared to the
beauty in your eyes.

RIYA
You're casting magic with your words.

EDWARD
But you...
you're the real witch,
you cast a spell every time you smile.

RIYA
What if I leave you?

EDWARD
If God takes you away from me...
I'll burn heaven down and turn it into hell.

RIYA
What do you think about love?

EDWARD
To me... love is hope.
And you... you are my hope.

They hold hands and look into each other's eyes. Riya smiles shyly and bites her lip, fixing her hair behind her ear. Her heart beats fast as she looks at him. Slowly, she leans in and kisses him

IT'S THE FIRST TIME THAT I AM FEELING THE WARMTH OF HER LIPS.

In The Parking Lot Morning

He is trying to start his e-bike it's running with
Kinetic energy but some malfunction

Come on what's wrong with you

Suddenly a car stopped

VICTOR
Need a ride

EDWARD
Hi, vector Well, doing great

VICTOR
If you're not coming I will break that scrap
that's not going to be great

EDWARD
Okay.. fine

VICTOR
Put that shit in back trunk

Car is moving...

Inside The Car

                    VICTOR
        That e-bike is not in use for a century

                    EDWARD
    I build it by myself paddling energy transform
    into kinetic energy I use it has a backup for
                my e-bike battery

                    VICTOR
    Rechargeable battery e-bike came many
            years ago and it's effective

                    EDWARD
    But it will consume more energy already we
    need more energy to run it's a free of cost
              and it' eco friendly

                    VICTOR
        You're not going to listen to me right

                    EDWARD
    You're not going to understand me right

Both are laughing.....

At The Beach Night

They speaking about their old memories in the school days

VICTOR
What happened to this place it last it's beautiful Guess, karma

VICTOR
Well... it's been a while

EDWARD
We have to do something

VICTOR
What...
We can't change the nature

Suddenly there was a red alarm buzzing in their mobile Strom alert they're seeing each other

VICTOR
Run....

EDWARD
Agree....

Edward and Victor are running through heavy rain and lightning, heading toward underground bunkers.

                    EDWARD
Oh no... we need to find an underground
                    bunker!

                    VICTOR
There's no time for that! Let's get inside this
                    shop!

                    EDWARD
Breaking into a shop? That's a crime!

                    VICTOR
We don't have a choice
                    help me!

They both break the shop door and rush inside.

Inside The Shop Night

A loud thunderclap. Lightning hits a terminal on a nearby building.
The current travels through underground pipes.

EDWARD
What just happened?

VICTOR
The lightning hit the terminal and traveled
through those pipes.

EDWARD
That's not what I meant. Where is it going?

VICTOR
It's not going anywhere.
It's just being redirected through pipes
underground, probably all the way to the
ocean under our feet.

EDWARD
Why aren't we converting it into electricity?

VICTOR
Turning lightning into electricity?
Great idea
Don't burn your ass

Sector 4 Night

The storm stops. People slowly come out of
hiding.

                    EDWARD
I'm serious. Why can't we convert lightning
            into electricity?

                    VICTOR
Because it's not possible. Lightning is a
massive burst of energy. No capacitor in
          the world can handle it.

                    EDWARD
Maybe we can invent something...

                    VICTOR
                    Sure.
Good luck,building that in your garage.
      Get home safe I'm out of here.

Edward 's House Midnight

Edward sits at a desk, researching. K1, an AI
assistant, helps him.

                    EDWARD
If lightning can travel through underground
pipes, maybe we can direct it through
            mainframes.

K1
That would be dangerous.
It could cause huge electrical explosions.

EDWARD
What if we split the lightning into smaller parts,
and store them in different capacitors?

K1
You can't break lightning. It's pure energy. You
can only transfer it into something else.

EDWARD
Exactly. If we transfer lightning into electricity,
maybe we can then divide the electricity safely.

K1
Theoretically possible... but no one has ever
created something like that.

EDWARD
Then we'll be the first to build it.

Edward and K1 try building a device. They fail
again and again.
Exhausted, they lie on the floor.

EDWARD
You know... I feel happy. With you. And... with
her.

K1
I'm glad to hear that.

EDWARD
Hey, buddy. Will you stay with me... forever?

K1
Until your last breath.

EDWARD
Yeah... the last breath... That's it, K1. You're a
genius!

K1
I didn't do anything.

EDWARD
We don't need to split the lightning. We can
redirect it into multiple transmitters at the
end.

K1
Right. Then, at the endpoint, the electricity
gets divided. Each transmitter can handle a
portion.

EDWARD
I need to write this down. We're building the
prototype.

Edward rushes to the table, grabs a diary, and
starts writing.

K1
A new era of technology is born here.
History will remember your name, sir.

In The Empty Ground Night

Edward and Victor are setting up a lightning
capture device. Edward is preparing his new
energy capacitor.

VICTOR
Edward , this is crazy! You're going to blow
everything up!

EDWARD
Just wait it's going to
work. Trust me.

VICTOR
You're trying to capture lightning?
Yeah, sure... I totally trust you. (nervously)

EDWARD
Look, I'll send the drone into the sky. When
lightning strikes, it'll hit the drone. The drone
will redirect the lightning to these transmitters,
and the energy will travel through the wires
and be stored in the capacitor.

VICTOR
Yeah, okay... I get it. Just don't blow your face
off.

Victor still scared

The sky darkens. A storm is approaching.

EDWARD
It's coming... look!

He is excited!

VICTOR
Oh no... Edward , get under the bridge!

EDWARD
Wait! I need to turn on the terminals.

Edward switches on the device and runs toward the bridge.
A bolt of lightning strikes. The drone captures it, redirects it to the terminals, and the electricity is stored in the capacitor. Victor watches, stunned.

EDWARD
Hey, look! It's working!

VICTOR
Yeah... you did it!

While Edward checks the device, Victor quietly sneaks over and steals Edward 's diary.

FEW DAYS LATER

Inside The House Of Edward Morning

Edward and K1 are preparing breakfast.

EDWARD
Not too spicy.

K1
Then I'll add some yogurt.

EDWARD
Yes, yogurt is good.

Edward   eats with his hand.

EDWARD
Today is an important day for me.

K1
Yes, I'm sure it is.

Mumbai City Morning

Edward walks through the street on his way to the Indian Institute of Technology.
As he passes a large building, a news report plays on a digital screen.

NEWS REPORTER (ON SCREEN)
Victor is now speaking about a new invention that produces electricity from lightning.

VICTOR (ON SCREEN)
Yes, this invention will create a new revolution. It's the result of my hard work for many years.

Edward watches in shock. His files fall from his hands.

Victor's House – Night

Victor stands in front of a mirror, drinking alcohol and talking to himself.
 Suddenly, Edward storms in.

                    EDWARD
                Victor! Victor!

                    VICTOR
            Calm down, my friend.

                    EDWARD
            That was my project...

                    VICTOR
    Not anymore. The government is funding
this project with millions. We'll be rich. I'll give
            you a good share.

                    EDWARD
        It's not fair. That's a crime.

VICTOR
Listen. "This world gives you two choices be a good person and struggle all your life, or become a villain and build a better life no matter what." What will you do?

EDWARD
No. I'm not listening to you. That project is mine.
I'm going to expose you.

Victor punches Edward and throws him out of the house. Edward runs into the street, bleeding from his nose and forehead. His nameplate falls behind him. He keeps running, terrified.

PRESENT TIME

Victor Industries Morning

Edward wakes up inside a healing pod.

K1
Sir, your body cells are dying.

EDWARD
So are my emotions...

K1
Sir, her DNA is a match.

EDWARD
Then it's time.

Edward   puts on his armor.

EDWARD
Wounds will heal scars will fade but it's hard
to forget the pain

PART 4: HOPE AND COURAGE

THUNDER MANIPULATION

LEVEL 6-HIGH MELTING POINT

Inside The House Of Meera Afternoon

Hope slowly wakes up and sees Meera and Yuva beside her

                    HOPE
                Where am I?

                    MEERA
        You're awake! We thought you were dead.

                    HOPE
                How did you find me?

                    YUVA
    I did. I got a message from someone unknown.
    He called himself ATG. I also saw your fight
                with that Terminator guy.

                    HOPE
    He was too powerful... He had powers like
                    mine.

                    MEERA
        I get it. He's a... supervillain.

YUVA
He destroyed all of Sector 2. We have to stop
him.

HOPE
No, you don't understand.
He was unstoppable.
I couldn't beat him... I was scared.

She starts crying

MEERA
It's okay.
You don't have to face him alone. We'll be
with you.

HOPE
But you can't help me. You don't have powers
like I do.

YUVA
That's where you're wrong. You don't need
powers to help someone. All you need is a
good heart and a willing mind.

MEERA
Exactly. Just like your father. It's okay to be
afraid.

HOPE
Thank you, Meera.

MEERA
Remember, you don't have to do everything by yourself. Sometimes, all you need is someone to push you forward.

Hope smiles through her tears

HOPE
Alright. What's the plan?

YUVA
First, you need to learn how to control your powers.

In The Road Of Mumbai City Evening

Hope is lifting weight

MEERA
Alright move, move, move

HOPE
That's not what I mean

MEERA
Shut up do what I say

Hope and Yuva are training together. Yuva is helping Hope learn to control her powers.

 She focuses hard, while Yuva guides her and cheers her on.

Far away, from the top of a tall building, someone is watching them through binoculars.

They stay hidden behind a broken wall, observing every move quietly.

Hope stands with lightning crackling softly in her hands. She looks at Yuva and smiles.

HOPE
"I'm naming it Thunder Manipulation,"

YUVA
"Nice. It suits you."

Together, Hope and Yuva create her power levels, giving each stage a name and testing her strength. They laugh and work as a team, learning more about her powers. But they don't know...someone is still watching from the building,

In The Road Of Mumbai City Night

Hope is sitting in the building, looking over the city.
Yuva quietly walks up behind her.

YUVA
I think you're thirsty. I brought some drinks.

HOPE
Thanks!

YUVA
It's okay.

HOPE
I'm sorry about that day... you took
those heavy punches for me.

YUVA
No need to say sorry.
Pretty good view, huh?

HOPE
Yeah. When I feel lonely, I come here.

YUVA
To relax?

HOPE
No... to take drugs.

YUVA
Wait, what?

He was surprised

HOPE
I know... I know it's wrong.

There is little awkward silence between them

YUVA
Hey, look. We all make mistakes.
Doing something bad doesn't make you a
bad person.Your past doesn't matter as
much as what you choose to do next.
Life gives us two choices
You can stay stuck in your past, keep hurting
yourself, and make things worse
Or you can let go and turn the page, start a new
chapter.
It's all in your hands.

 Yuva walks away, leaving Hope deep in
thought.

In The Road Of Mumbai City Morning

Hope is walking down the street with a bag of
groceries in her hand. She suddenly feels
someone following her.

She quickly turns a corner, hides, and waits. As
the person walks by, she grabs and pins him
against the wall. It's Jeeva.

HOPE
Why are you following me?

JEEVA
I... I couldn't breathe.
I saw some electrical sparks,
coming from your hands.

HOPE
How long have you been following me?

JEEVA
For a long time...

She was shocked

HOPE
Wait... you're ATG?

Before he can answer, a loud blast happens nearby. Hope's heart starts racing. The smoke clears, and Edward appears.

EDWARD
I finally found you.

Jeeva is smirking

JEEVA
This just got interesting...

She is backing away and turns to Edward

                    HOPE
            Stay back, Jeeva.
          It's time for a rematch.

                   EDWARD
           No one can beat me.

Hope tries to fight him, but Edward dodges her attack. He pulls out an electromagnetic gun and fires. A powerful shock hits Hope. Her powers disappear.

She falls to her knees, weak.

                    HOPE
           What did you do to me?

                   EDWARD
          Our shared weakness...

He grabs her and flies away. Jeeva watches, frozen.

                   JEEVA
                   Great.
        Now, I have to warn those two idiots.

He starts walking casually toward a large group in the distance.

Inside The Victor Industries Morning

Hope slowly wakes up. She realizes she's inside a glass box. Her hands and legs are tied. She struggles to break free but can't.

K1
Don't worry. We're not going to hurt you. We just need a few samples.

HOPE
I don't believe you! Let me out! Where is that freak?

K1
You don't know anything about him.

Hope turns her head and sees another glass box.

Riya is inside, preserved and unmoving. She starts to panic, sensing that something bad is going to happen.

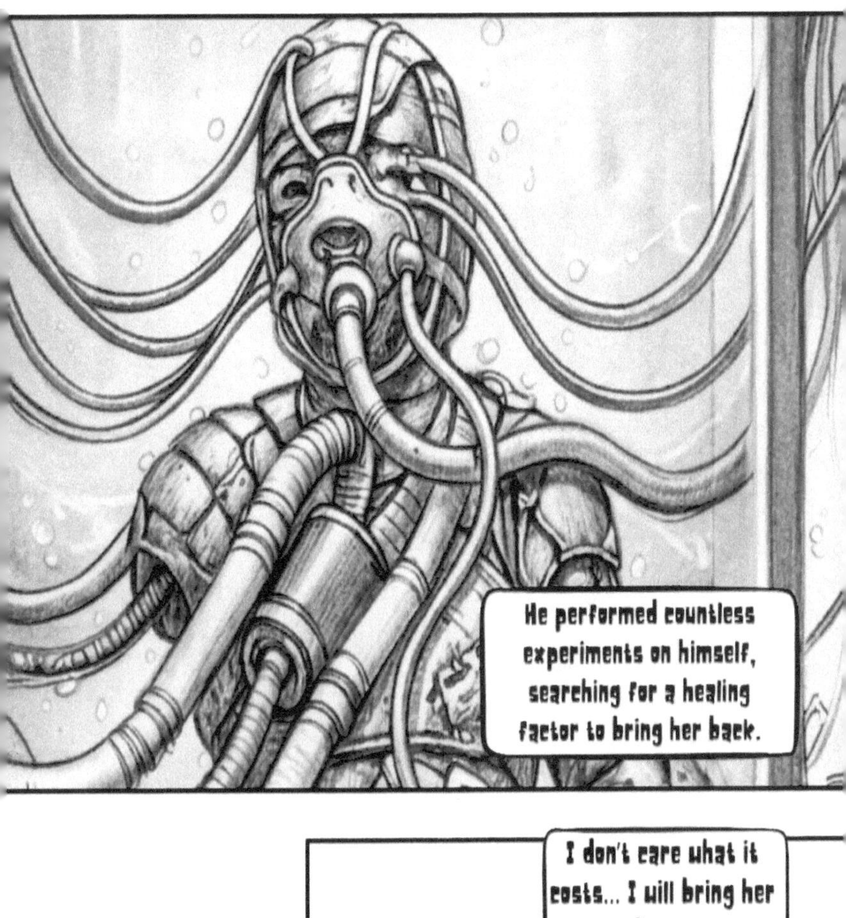

He performed countless experiments on himself, searching for a healing factor to bring her back.

I don't care what it costs... I will bring her back.

'Nothing worked. His body was slowly failing, his organs shutting down one by one."

Empty Ground – Evening

Meera and Yuva are waiting for Hope to show up for training.

MEERA
Why is she taking so long to get here?

YUVA
Maybe because you scared her off with your tough training.

MEERA
I'm going to double her training next time.

Suddenly, Jeeva appears, running up to them.

JEEVA
She's not coming. She was kidnapped.

YUVA
What?!

MEERA
That's not possible!

JEEVA
I saw it with my own eyes. He took her to

Victor Industries.

YUVA
Wait... how do you even know about us?

JEEVA
Well, she covered her face, but you two didn't.
It wasn't hard to figure it out.

MEERA
I didn't think of that...

YUVA
Then why didn't you help her?

JEEVA
Right, like I'd fight someone who can destroy
the whole world. Sounds smart, huh?

MEERA
Then what do we do now? Any ideas?

JEEVA
I've got one. Follow me!

They all start heading toward the Victor
Industries building.

Inside The Victor Industries Evening

Edward is waking up inside a healing pod. He looks weak and worse than before.

                    KI
Sir, I've assembled everything just like you said.

                    EDWARD
                    Good...

Hope struggles in her restraints.
Edward starts setting up the machines.

                    HOPE
            Hey... hey! Look at me!

                    EDWARD
        We're going to take her bone marrow.

                    KI
Sir, she will die! I thought you were only going to take some samples.

                    EDWARD
            There's no time for that.

KI looks confused. He glances at hope.

HOPE
Let me out!

EDWARD
Be quiet.

HOPE
Why are you doing this? What do you want
from me?

EDWARD
I need something from you that I don't have.

HOPE
You want my powers?

EDWARD
Not just your power
something more.

HOPE
Let me go.
I can give you more than you think.

EDWARD
You little punk. You think you're a superhero
saving people from trouble?
But the moment you mess up, the world will
turn against you.

Meera, Yuva, and Jeeva have entered the
building.
They're looking for .

HOPE
You're a bad person.

EDWARD
No one is good or bad in this cursed world.
Everyone is just... fucking selfish.

HOPE
Not everyone.
My father saved many lives.

EDWARD
So? Is he alive now?

HOPE
He gave his life to save children!

EDWARD
See? That's exactly my point.

HOPE
No, you don't get it! He chose to help others.
He was brave and selfless!

EDWARD
Say whatever you want. You're going to die
anyway.

He pulls a lever. A needle moves toward her
spine.
Hope screams in pain.

Suddenly, Meera rushes in and throws a book
at Edward .

MEERA
Hey! Leave my friend alone!

While Meera and Yuva distract him, Jeeva
sneaks over to rescue. He moves carefully.

MEERA
He's coming closer! Do something!

She hides behind yuva.

YUVA
No way! Ladies first.

He hides behind her.

MEERA
Oh no...
Do something! I'm the only child at home I
don't want to die!

EDWARD
You little insects...

Suddenly, the machine stops. Jeeva has freed
Hope.

JEEVA
Oh no... I'm so dead!

EDWARD
You little brat!

Edward gets furious and shoots laser beams
from his eyes. He tries to burn Jeeva.

But KI steps in and hits Edward   with an
electromagnetic   pulse.   Edward   falls,
powerless.

EDWARD
Why?

KI
Sir, I thought you were going to collect samples.
But you tried to kill her!

EDWARD
Obey me...

KI
You programmed me to help people, not harm them.

EDWARD
I... I need her. I can bring her back!

KI
Yes, you can... but at what cost?
Killing an innocent person?
She's already gone. Sometimes we need to stop and think about what's right and wrong. What you're doing is wrong. I can't let you continue.

FLASH BACK

In The Road Of Sector 2 Night

A man wearing a white lab coat stood in the street. Tears were running down his face. He was shaking as he wiped the blood from his nose. He looked tired and hurt.

Someone was coming closer.

He slowly looked up.

It was Riya.

She had tears in her eyes. She ran to him and knelt down in front of him. Gently, she touched his face.

                    RIYA
            "Edward ... look at me,"

She pulled him into a hug, holding him close like she didn't want to let go.

                    RIYA
      "It's going to be okay. I promise. Let's go
                    home."

PRESENT TIME

Inside The Victor Industries Evening

He thinks about her memories.

EDWARD
I loved her.

Meera, Yuva, and Jeeva reunite. They still have hope, but she is unconscious.

YUVA
"Love makes even the strongest man into the weakest. It's sad."

JEEVA
Did I ask for a poem, Run you idiots?

K1 tries to stop Edward.
Meanwhile Meera, Yuva, and Jeeva try to escape, carrying the unconscious girl. Meera and Yuva grab her and run toward the exit.

Edward grabs an electric wire nearby. He becomes powerful again. He punches K1 with super speed.

K1 tries to hit him with an electromagnetic pulse, but Edward breaks his arm and makes a hole in his chest.

EDWARD
Don't worry. I'll fix you.

K1
Nothing is permanent. Some things can't be fixed.

K1 activates the building's self, destruction mode.

K1
Till your last breath!

Edward is shocked. He tries to save Riya, but suddenly there's a huge blast. The building collapses.

In The Road Of Mumbai City Evening

Meera, Yuva, and Jeeva were carrying Hope on their shoulders. They tried to run away from that place. Suddenly, there was a big explosion in the building.

Everyone on the street started to panic. They looked at each other, and Jeeva tried to say something.

MEERA
I don't want to hear anything.
Just take us to a safe place.

At The Top Of The Building

Hope was still unconscious. She had big wounds on her back and was bleeding a lot. They tried to wake her up, but it did not work.

MEERA
What do we do? We have to help her.

JEEVA
I have a crazy idea.

YUVA
Trust me. We have seen worse things than this.

Yuva and Jeeva broke the lightning antenna and took many wires. They wanted to give Hope an electric shock to wake her up.

JEEVA
He used a machine that stopped the electricity
in her body.

YUVA
What do you mean? Please explain without
hard words.

JEEVA
She is like a battery with no power. We will
charge her with electricity.

MEERA
What are you trying to do to my friend?

JEEVA
Well, a few minutes ago,
that man tried to kill me.

Meera looked at Hope with worry.

YUVA
We have no choice.

MEERA
Sorry, Hope. This will hurt.

They put wires on her body. Jeeva connected the wires to the power source and to Hope.

Electricity went through her body. She woke up and screamed in pain. Jeeva tried to stop, but Hope took all the electricity.

Her body started to heal. Her eyes and body began to shine with yellow light. Yellow sparkles came from her fingers.

YUVA
Stop now!

JEEVA
I am trying!

MEERA
Do something!

The electric shock made Hope remember her past with her father. She took all the energy, and the antenna broke. Then she woke up fully.

MEERA
Hope...

HOPE
What happened?

YUVA
Nothing much.
We just gave you an electric shock.

HOPE
You did what?

JEEVA
Yes, that was my crazy idea.

HOPE
What happened? I don't remember. That man
tried to kill me.

In The Blast Area Evening

The whole building fell down.
Edward came out of the broken building. His
leg and arm were hurt. He had a ring that Riya
gave him.

He opened a small electric capsule in his hand. It gave him power. His broken body started to heal. He grabbed an electric wire nearby and took all the energy from it.

While taking the energy, his old memories came back.

EDWARD
I just wanted to make the world better.
But I can't even fix my own life.
She was a good person.
If she didn't deserve to live...
Then no one does.
What's the point of this world?
I'm going to burn it all down.

He went crazy. He broke the floor and went inside the building.
He wore his armor. Now he looked very angry and very strong.
He punched a nearby building. It fell down.

People screamed and ran away.

On Top Of A Building

Everyone watched the building fall.

HOPE
He's not dead. He came back.

MEERA
What do we do now?

YUVA
We must stop him. He will hurt people.

JEEVA
Oh wow. Great idea. I'll bring flowers to your graves.

YUVA
Then tell me, who else will stop him?

JEEVA
Not us. We should run and stay safe. Hope looked at the people running below. The others kept talking.

HOPE
I'm not going anywhere. I'll fight him.

JEEVA
That's too dangerous! You'll die. We saved you once already.

HOPE
I know. But I can't leave these people.

YUVA
I won't leave them either.

MEERA
I'm always with you, Hope.

JEEVA
You three never listen to me, huh?

HOPE
Okay, so what's the plan?

JEEVA
I have another crazy idea. But I need help
from all of you.

MEERA
Looks like we're becoming super, duper
heroes now! Like Avengers

JEEVA
Shut up!

YUVA
You can't say that word

In The Road Of Sector 4 Night

A man looks at the broken building. He sees
something moving.

Edward walks out from the dust and fire.

EDWARD
Don't be scared. I'm not a bad
person. I only wanted a
peaceful life... But look at what
I've become.

He looks at his hands. They have blood on
them.
He gives the man a scary look.

EDWARD
I became... death.

He grabs the man's head and crushes it.
Then he starts killing everyone with his super
speed and laser beams.

He hears a train underground.
He breaks the ground and jumps in.
A train is coming.
He smashes the train.
The broken train crashes out onto the street.
 People scream and run away.
Edward grabs someone's neck and tries to kill.
Just then, Hope arrives.

HOPE
Let them go!

He breaks the man's neck and throws him like dust.
Hope looks scared.

Edward walks toward her.
The ground shakes.

Lights flicker.
Blue sparks come from his armor.
His eyes glow blue.

HOPE
Stop!
You are killing too many innocent people!

                    EDWARD
                    Innocent?
                They are like bugs.
            They don't deserve to live.

                     HOPE
               What do you want?

                    EDWARD
                  What I want...
              You can never give me.

                     HOPE
               Then I will stop you!

                    EDWARD
                  Then come.
               Fight to the death.

Edward   runs at her with super speed. The air
shakes.
He punches her hard. She falls and slides on
the ground.

Hope stands up fast.
Her hands spark with electricity.

She tries to hit him
But he's already gone.

Too fast.

HOPE
"You're too fast!"

He smiles and says,

EDWARD
"Then stop me if you can."

Then, he lifts his hand. Electrical sparks comes out from his hand, shooting across the air and hitting the ground near Hope. The light is bright, and the power is strong.

Hope is shocked.

His hand glows with blue electricity. He uses his
Energy Manipulation

Hope takes a deep breath. She shouts,

HOPE
"Thunder Manipulation, Level 2! – Thunder blast"

Her body lights up with power. Electrical energy projection to hit him and he throws metal objects at her. She blocks the metal and blasts him with a wave of thunder. He slides back but doesn't fall.

He laughs.

EDWARD
"Not bad. But now it's my turn."

He lifts his hand again. This time, the lightning in his palm grows stronger and brighter.

EDWARD
"Energy Manipulation, Level 3-Bright light"

The energy is loud and wild. Hope powers up too.
Sparks cover her body. She runs toward him.

He runs at her.

Boom! Their powers crash into each other.
Lightning flies in all directions.
Thunder shakes the ground.

They keep fighting, both using all their power levels..
Neither of them gives up.

In The Top Of The Building Night

MEERA
Okay she fights with devil what is the plan?

JEEVA
There major weakness his EMP, we have to create one large amount electromagnetic pulse that will make him weaker.

YUVA
Okay, what I have to do for you?

JEEVA
Can you see this signal tower you have to go there and place this electromagnet,
I will go inside the building to start the antenna from main frames.

MEERA
It's middle of the war he will die.

YUVA
Don't worry, Meera nothing is going to happen,
I'm on,

MEERA
What i have to do?

YUVA
Take this binoculars ,
your are the one who is going to guide us, give
signal in a perfect time,

Meera hugs both of them

MEERA
I'm so proud of you two.

YUVA
Thanks!

JEEVA
Get your hands out form me

Yuva and jeeva going separately Meera looks
everyone with her binoculars hope is
struggling to fight with Edward

MEERA
Poor hope....

Hope and Edward   are still fighting. Lightning flashes. Thunder is loud. Both are using their powers.

Suddenly, Hope gets scared.
Her hands are shaking. She is breathing fast. Her powers grow weak. Her eyes show fear.

He sees it.

In one quick move, he runs to her and grabs her head with one hand. She can't move.

His eyes glow bright. His voice is quiet but scary.

EDWARD
"I can still hear your heartbeat..."

Before she can fight back, he throws her into a building.

The wall breaks. Hope crashes through it. Dust and glass fall everywhere.

She slowly gets up. Her body hurts. The building is dark, full of broken things.

She starts to run.

But he's already inside. He keeps stopping her.

Hope's breath is fast. Small sparks come from her hands. But she's afraid.

He walks closer. Then everything goes quiet.

He lifts both hands. Bright blue lightning glows from his fingers. The air feels hot.

EDWARD
"Energy Manipulation, Level 4-Blue current"

The power grows. The lights flicker. The walls shake.

BOOM!

He blasts all the lightning at once.

The building explodes.
Windows break.
Walls fall.

The roof crashes down.

Hope is thrown backward. She covers herself with her power, trying to survive.

The whole building falls to the ground. Smoke and fire rise into the sky.

And in the middle of it all, he is standing... lightning crackling around him... fire behind him... And on his face... a slow, creepy smile.

Like he's enjoying every second of it.

In The Top Of The Building Night

Meera is watching Yuva climb the antenna. They are talking using earbuds. Yuva looks back and sees people fighting and destroying buildings.

MEERA
You're doing great!

YUVA
That's not very helpful.

MEERA
You need to go a little higher. He's putting
the electromagnet on the tower.

YUVA
Okay, I'm almost there.

Inside The Signal Tower Night

Yuva turns on all the switches. The building
starts shaking because of the fight outside.

JEEVA
I'm going to increase the frequency of the
tower. It will affect your brain, so get out
quickly!

Top Of The Building Night

YUVA
Okay, I got it!

Inside The Signal Tower Night

Jeeva increases the frequency. The building
starts to break because of the fight.

JEEVA
Oh no...

He runs to the exit.

On the Road Night

The two enemies are fighting in the air, punching each other.

Top Of The Building Antenna Tower

A big electromagnetic wave hits both fighters. Their powers stop working. They fall down.

MEERA
Yes! We did it!

One of them sees the tower. He uses an electric capsule and becomes powerful again. He shoots a laser beam at the tower. The building crashes into another one.

YUVA
Oh no...

Meera is shocked.

MEERA
What do we do now?

Yuva hears a child crying. He sees a broken building and a child hanging from it.

CHILD
Help me!

YUVA
Hold on, kid! I'm coming!

Yuva sees a ladder and makes a bridge to the other building. The child is about to fall.

Yuva runs on the ladder and grabs the child's hand just in time. He holds the child with one hand and hangs onto a metal pipe with the other.

A brick hits Yuva's head. He starts bleeding. The child cries loudly.

YUVA
Don't worry. I won't let you fall.

In The Road Of Mumbai City Night

Hope felt weak and dizzy after the EMP attack. She could not see clearly. Suddenly, he came close and grabbed her neck.

He flew up into the sky, holding her tightly. Then, without warning, he let her go.

Hope fell from the sky and hit the ground hard. She cried out in pain. Her body hurt, but she tried to stand up.

Before she could, he landed near her. He hit her with his knee, and she fell again. Then he started punching her face again and again.

Her face began to bleed. Her skin broke. She looked badly hurt.
Meera, Yuva, and Jeeva saw everything. They stood still, shocked. A few other people were there too. Everyone was looking at Hope.
Some had tears in their eyes. Others looked scared and sad.

Hope was bleeding, but she was still alive. She was still trying to fight.

MEERA
Hope...

She is crying

His each punches cause a large amount of
sound travels across the street her heart beat
Started to slow down

JEEVA
She needs to grab some electricity...

Her heart beat stops

FLASH BACK

In The Playground Evening

Hope is little child Playing with her father she
wants to climb up the rope ladder but she was
frightened by the height she staring at the
ladder.

HOPE'S FATHER
Do you want climbed up?

HOPE
I want to climb up

HOPE'S FATHER
Then why are you still staring at the ladder go
on

HOPE
I was afraid...I will fall

Hope father laughs and holds her shoulders

HOPE'S FATHER
Look hope bravery is not about acting as
your fearless
The real courage is when you know it's going
to hurt you but you will still fights for what you
want Trust yourself hope if you trust yourself
one day you will become hope to everyone

HOPE
I didn't get it

HOPE'S FATHER
One day you will understand this words and
you will climb this ladder
Okay little soldier did you ready to kill the
peanut monster

HOPE'S FATHER
Let's kill the peanut monster

HOPE
Yeah....

Hope father takes a gun toy and puts helmet in
her head they are playing in the garden

Let's kill the peanut monster
Yeah.....

PRESENT TIME

In The Road Of Mumbai City Night

Edward kept punching Hope's face again and again. He tried to hit her one more time.

But Hope stopped his hand with her left hand.

The armor on his arm started to shake and crack.

Then, Hope kicked him hard in the chest.

Edward flew back and crashed into a nearby building. The wall broke as he hit it.

Hope slowly stood up. Her eyes started to glow yellow.

Yellow sparkles came out from her whole body. She was floating in the air.

Edward came out of the broken building. He looked angry.
He shot a laser beam at her.

Hope's eyes glowed brighter, in golden, yellow color. A laser beam came out from her eyes too.

The two laser beams hit each other.

The light was very strong. The metal around them started to melt.

EDWARD
"Die!"

He is screaming

He ran very fast and tried to punch her again.

But Hope moved fast and missed the punch.

They started fighting at super speed.

Jeeva watched from far away. He looked shocked.

JEEVA
"They are faster than sound!"

Hope flew up into the air. Her body was glowing.

Then she shouted loudly

HOPE
Thunder Manipulation Level 5- Thunder Punch

In The Top Of The Building

Meera was watching everything through her binoculars. Her hands were shaking as she followed the fight in the sky.

Suddenly, her phone rang. The screen turned red and flashed with a warning.

She looked at it, confused. Then she heard a loud rumble behind her.

She turned around.

Dark clouds were gathering fast. A huge thunderstorm was coming.

MEERA
"Oh no... not now..."

She ran inside the building to take cover.

Outside, the wind howled. Lightning struck the ground. The thunderstorm hit the area with full force.

But Edward and Hope kept fighting in the middle of the storm.

A bolt of lightning hit both of them at the same time.

The energy made them even more powerful.

They flew toward each other at top speed and punched each other hard.

ENERGY MANIPULATION

THUNDER MANIPULATION

BOOM!

A huge explosion happened on the street. The shockwave was so strong that it broke windows and pushed cars away.

Both of them were thrown out by the blast.

Edward 's armor was damaged. Parts of it were broken and burning.

He stood up and tried to fight again, but he was weak now.

Hope was too strong.

Edward flew up into the sky, trying to escape.

But Hope followed him. She rose slowly through the dark clouds, her body glowing like a sun.

"I CAN HEAR YOUR HEARTBEAT... WHAT HAPPENED? AFRAID?"

HOPE
"I can hear your heartbeat... What happened?
Afraid?"

Lightning flashed around her. Then she raised her hands to the sky.

She began to absorb all the lightning from the clouds. Every spark, every bolt entered her body.

Her eyes, mouth, and even her skin started glowing golden yellow.

HOPE
Thunder Manipulation Level 6-
High melting point.

 Her power was now at the highest point.

Her skin became super hot,
Hot enough to melt steel. Her body reached a high melting point.
Edward rushed toward her and tried to punch.

But Hope was faster.
She charged her fist with lightning and punched him right in the chest.

BOOM!!!

There was a massive blast in the sky. The clouds split apart. Light filled the sky.

Edward was thrown far away, his armor completely destroyed, his body falling fast.

Hope also fell from the sky. Her eyes closed as she lost all her energy.

As she fell, she remembered her father's words

HOPE'S FATHER
Remember hope you may fall from the heights it will hurt you but don't forget to get up
Even if you fall , fall like a thunder

Hope wakes up in the air.
She closes her fist and punches the ground.
Yellow sparks spread across the street.
She slowly stands up.
The sun is rising.

RANDOM PERSON
That little girl saved us!

Yuva comes out of the building with a child.
The child runs to his mother.

                    CHILD
                    Momma!

The child points at Yuva.

                    CHILD
                Momma... superhero!

                CHILD'S MOTHER
                    Thank you...

Yuva smiles. These words make him feel happy.

On top of a building – Morning

Hope flies and lands near Meera.
They hug each other.

                    JEEVA
                I thought you were dead!

HOPE
Yes, for a moment…
But now, I can control my powers.

JEEVA
That's good. So no more practice sessions?

MEERA
Are you okay?

YUVA
Yeah, It's just a small injury.

JEEVA
Small? It could get infected! Your skin could
rot, and you could die in pain!

Yuva looks shocked. Everyone laughs.

On The Streets Of Mumbai Morning

Rescue teams are helping people.
Hope walks slowly toward her house.
Her mother sees her and runs to her with tears.

HOPE
Sorry, I

Her mother hugs her, crying.
Hope hugs her back with a smile and tears.

Inside Hope's House Morning

A news reporter is talking on TV.

NEWS REPORTER
We still don't know who they are.
Some say they are aliens.
Some say they are demons.
But one thing is sure
We are not alone in this universe.

Hope and her mother are doing housework.
Hope gets ready to leave for school.

HOPE'S MOTHER
Bye, Hope. Go safely.

HOPE
Yeah, you too. Bye, Mom!

Outside Of The Class

Everyone is comforting each other after everything that happened. The mood is a little better now.

                    HOPE
I think they've all changed.

                    MEERA
          Yeah, I can see that.

She looks at Hope's face and smiles.

In the corner, Robert is showing off to a group of girls.

               ROBERT CLIVE
 I was right in the middle of the fight. He
 grabbed my neck, I punched him in the face
 and boom! He was gone!

The girls laugh loudly.

                    MEERA
       That guy will never change.

Jeeva is sitting alone in another corner, reading a book. Hope walks over to him.

HOPE
Hey…

JEEVA
Sorry. I know you're always curious about things… But I'm not going to tell you anything about your powers.
Bye.

HOPE
Wait…
I just wanted to say thank you.
For helping me.

He was surprised

JEEVA
You're not mad at me?

HOPE
No. Why would I be?

They look at each other for a moment.

                         JEEVA
          Your superhero suit is a little torn.
                    I can help fix it.

She is blushing

                          HOPE
                        Thanks...

Jeeva gets shy and walks away.

Suddenly, Yuva walks into the room. Everyone turns to look at him.

He looks nervous, thinking they'll tease him. He starts walking to his class quietly.

                         JASON
                  Hey! Look who's here!

Yuva looks at Jason nervously. Jason grins and lifts Yuva onto his shoulder.

                         JASON
                 He saved a little child.
Everyone starts clapping and cheering loudly.

Crowd....Yuva!.... Yuva!... Yuva!....

Robert watches his group of girls run toward Yuva to celebrate.

ROBERT
Hey! Girls, don't go! I was still talking!

The girls ignore him and keep cheering with the crowd. Robert stands there, fake heartbroken.

ROBERT
Every time someone becomes a
hero, I lose my audience.

JEEVA
After all, barbarians have brains too

Hope and Meera laugh as they watch everything unfold.

MEERA
He really deserves that moment.

She is Smiling

HOPE
Yeah...

Hope and Meera start walking toward their class.

MEERA
Let's go eat lunch somewhere safe.
No supervillains. Just food.

HOPE
Yes please! I'm super hungry!

They both laugh and walk off together.

In the top of the building evening

Hope sits on the edge of a tall building.
She wears her new superhero costume with a black suit with golden lines and a hood covering her head.

She looks at the city below.
Many buildings are broken.
The streets are quiet.
Everything was destroyed during the fight.

She takes out a small photo from her
pocket A picture of her and her father.

She looks at it for a moment... then starts to
cry.
Tears fall from her eyes as she remembers the
happy times with her dad
His smile, his voice, and the way he used to
hold her hand.

She wipes her tears slowly.

Softly, to herself

HOPE
I'll make you proud, Dad...

She looks at the photo one last time, then puts
it back inside her suit.

She stands up, with the wind blowing through
her hoodie, and looks at the rising sun. with
her hand

HOPE
I'm not going to cry anymore

She wears her mask and she jumps from the building she flies all the way towards the Taj Mahal

                    HOPE
            I AM THUNDER GIRL

Outer Space

After the big fight between Edward   and Hope...

Hope punches Edward   hard in the chest.
The power of the punch sends him flying into space.

His armor is broken.
He has lost one hand and one leg.
He is still alive, but his heartbeat is getting slower.

Suddenly, he sees Riya flying toward him. She looks like a blue angel, glowing in the dark space.
She gently holds his face.

(with tears)

I'M
RRY..

LET'S GO
HOME...

EDWARD
I'm sorry...

RIYA
Let's go home...

But then she disappears.
It was just a memory or a dream.
Edward remembers something Riya asked
him before

RIYA (in memory)
What do you think about love?

EDWARD (in memory)
What is love?
Love is a curse...

Now, his heart finally stops.
His hand opens.

Riya's ring floats away from him, slowly
spinning in space.

THE END?

Even If You Fall,

HOPE

CHAPTER 2: GOD'S AND MONSTER'

SURIYA.B

Fall Like Thunder